Super Pig
and
Jip the pirate

Illustrated by

Nina O'Connell

Nelson

Super Pig

"Look at me.
I am Super Pig.
I am going to Deb's party."
Pat the pig sat down to wait
for Sam and Meg.
He went to sleep. Zzzzzzz.

"Look at me.
What can I see?
I can see Sam.
I will help him.
I am Super Pig."

3

"Look at me.

What can I see?

Jip is in the fire.

I will help him.

Here comes Super Pig."

"Look at me.
What can I see?
I can see Ben.
I will help him.
I am Super Pig."

"Look at me.
I can see Deb.
I can help Deb, too.
I am Super Pig."

"What can I see now?
There is Meg.
I will help her.
Here comes Super Pig."

"Come on, Pat.
Get up.
It is time to go
to Deb's party."

Jip the pirate

Jip was going to Deb's party.

"I will be a pirate," he said.

"I will have a red coat.

I will have a big hat.

I will have big boots."

Jip sat down to wait for
Pat and Ben and Meg.
He went to sleep.
Zzzzzz. Zzzzzz. Zzzzzz.

Jip was on a pirate ship.

The ship had a pirate flag.

The pirates had a map.

They wanted to find the gold.

"Where is the gold?" said Jip.

"I don't know," said Meg.

"You must ask Ben."

"Where is the gold?" said Jip.

"I don't know," said Ben.

"You must ask Pat."

"Where is the gold?" said Jip.

"I don't know," said Pat.

"Then you must walk the plank," said Jip.

Pat the pig got on the plank.

"Go on. Go on," said Jip.

Pat was just going to

fall into the water . . .

Bang. Bang. Bang.

"Come on, Jip," said Meg.

"Get up.

It is time to go to the party."